TWELVE DAYS OF CHRISTMAS HORROR VOLUME 2

RICK WOOD

RICK WOOD

Rick Wood is a British writer born in Cheltenham.

His love for writing came at an early age, as did his battle with mental health. After defeating his demons, he grew up and became a stand-up comedian, then a drama and English teacher, before giving it all up to become a full-time author.

He now lives in Loughborough, where he divides his time between watching horror, reading horror, and writing horror.

ALSO BY RICK WOOD

The Sensitives
The Sensitives
My Exorcism Killed Me
Close to Death
Demon's Daughter
Questions for the Devil
Repent
The Resurgence
Until the End

Blood Splatter Books
Psycho B*tches
Shutter House
This Book is Full of Bodies
Home Invasion
Haunted House
Woman Scorned

Cia Rose
When the World Has Ended
When the End Has Begun
When the Living Have Lost
When the Dead Have Decayed

The Edward King Series
I Have the Sight
Descendant of Hell
An Exorcist Possessed
Blood of Hope
The World Ends Tonight

Anthologies
Twelve Days of Christmas Horror
Twelve Days of Christmas Horror Volume 2
Roses Are Red So Is Your Blood

Standalones
When Liberty Dies
The Death Club

Sean Mallon
The Art of Murder
Redemption of the Hopeless

Chronicles of the Infected
Zombie Attack
Zombie Defence
Zombie World

Non-Fiction
How to Write an Awesome Novel
The Writer's Room

Rick also publishes thrillers under the pseudonym Ed Grace...
Jay Sullivan
Assassin Down
Kill Them Quickly
The Bars That Hold Me
A Deadly Weapon

© Copyright Rick Wood 2020

Cover design by bloodsplatterpress.com

With thanks to my Street Team.

No part of this book may be reproduced without express permission from the author.

THE PRESENT: THE FIRST CHRISTMAS

I haven't always loved Christmas.

In fact, there was a time I despised it.

In the fifteen years between being a child and becoming a parent, Christmas lost its magic. As a boy, the excitement leading up to Christmas morning was palpable. I looked forward to Santa arriving, the presents laid out in the morning, the mince pie for breakfast, the family games – it was a wondrous season.

Then I grew up, learned that Santa was a load of shit, and Christmas lost its soul.

Presents weren't even exciting anymore; anything I wanted, I could now afford. That DVD player, that television, that computer game; anything I might ask for I already have.

In my twenties, I'd visit my parents and siblings, we'd exchange a few gifts, have dry turkey and pull Christmas crackers and wear the annoying paper hat that doesn't fit my head, and it would be Christmas – but not like it was when I was younger. Christmas became something that came around every year, like my eye check-up, or my annual review at work, or my MOT. December would arrive and I'd think, *huh, it's Christmas again,* and I'd listen to the songs and watch the movies and try and get back into it, but even *Home Alone* wasn't the same.

Because I wasn't like Kevin McAllister anymore. I'm

often in the house alone and, should any robbers try to break in, I would get the hell out of there.

Then I met my wife. We had a child. And we told that child that, every 24th December, once they've gone to bed, a fat man in red squeezes down the chimney and leaves them presents. The excitement in their eyes on Christmas morning, their enthusiasm as they rip away the wrapping paper, the happiness when they spend all day playing with their toys – suddenly it feels like Christmas again.

I'm no longer just experiencing the magic; I am *creating* it.

And now I look forward to it every year. I start buying the presents as early as September, seeing things in toy shops that I know my son would like and being unable to stop myself from buying them. I pile them up in the cupboard, hardly able to contain my excitement for when I can watch him unwrap them and see his face light up.

And this Christmas morning is no different. Myself, my wife, Linda, and my son, Bobby, say goodnight on Christmas Eve, and go to bed. Once Bobby is asleep, Linda and I collect the presents and sneak them into the living room, placing them carefully and particularly.

When Bobby leaps on our bed and wakes us up in the morning, I am not angry like I would be any other day. I am excited – it's Christmas! Yay!

"Can we see if he's been?" Bobby says. "Can we? Can we?"

"You know the routine," I tell him. "Wait at the top of the stairs while we get ready."

And so he finds his place on the top step, rocking as he tries to restrain himself. He can see the living room door from where he sits, and I know he'll be staring at it, waiting to see what's behind it.

Linda and I take a little more time getting out of bed, just to prolong the anticipation. When we finally tell Bobby he can go downstairs, he leaps to his feet and runs down the stairs two steps at a time. And oh, his face as he enters! Gazing at all the presents left out for him, spread across the carpet, from the tree to the fireplace: large boxes, small boxes, tubes, soft rectangular shapes, some that rattle when you shake them, and some that make no sound.

Bobby barely knows where to start.

"Wow!" he exclaims.

"Looks like you've been a good boy this year," I tell him.

He nods, surveying the multicoloured wrappings, trying to decide where to start.

He dives to his feet and tears open the first one. It's a Star Wars action figure, one that had been at the top of the list he'd sent to Santa, and he turns back to us with a huge grin on his face.

The next present is a pair of Aladdin pyjamas that he looks at and discards – though I know he'll definitely be wanting to wear them tonight.

He goes through them all, one by one, finding sweets, toys, games, DVDs, books, and more toys and more games.

Within half an hour, half of the room is covered in ripped wrapping paper, and the other half is covered in gifts.

But there is one more. A large box beside the tree.

"What's this one?" Bobby asks. "It's huge!"

I look at Linda, assuming it's one that she bought, but she appears as equally perplexed as me. It's in red and gold wrapping paper that hasn't been used on any other present.

"Did you get that one?" I ask, under my breath, ensuring Bobby doesn't hear.

She shakes her head.

I stare at the present. Who is it from then? I don't remember bringing it down, though I did place the presents in the room so enthusiastically that I wasn't particularly paying attention.

Still, it seems strange that it is in different wrapping paper to the rest, and that neither of us can remember it.

"Why don't you find out?" I say, curious to find out myself; as soon as I see what it is, I am sure I will remember buying it.

"It's not fully wrapped," Bobby points out, and he's right – the box and the lid are wrapped separately, and he manages to lift the lid slightly without having to tear into anything.

"What is it?" I say, desperate to know.

With a huge grin at us, Bobby peers inside.

He says nothing.

Just stares.

"Bobby?"

Still nothing, just staring.

"Bobby, what is it?"

His body is still. At first, he looks perplexed, then his face empties of emotion. A tear rolls down his cheek, but his eyes are wide-open and he is otherwise motionless.

"Bobby?"

It's like he's in a trance.

I don't understand it.

"Bobby, what's the matter?"

Slowly, he closes the lid and stands still.

The happiness, the enthusiasm, the eagerness, it's all gone – and he stands rigidly, staring straight ahead whilst staring at nothing.

"Bobby? Bobby, you're scaring me, what is it?"

What could possibly have caused this reaction?

I go to look at the present, but he places his hand on top of it, turns to me, and screams the most rabid, animalistic scream I've ever heard. The sheer force of it is enough to send me onto my back, crawling away from him.

"Bobby, what–"

He turns. Runs out of the room.

I glance at Linda and we both go after him.

He's running quickly, perhaps too quickly, we can't keep up with him, and he goes into the kitchen, into the living room, into the study, and back into the hallway again.

Just as I think I'm about to grab him, he runs upstairs, into his bedroom, and slams the door.

We try to enter his room, but the door won't budge. Something is stopping it from opening.

There is a pounding coming from behind the door, each slam about two seconds apart, sinister and methodical.

"Bobby!" I shout, trying to open the door. "Bobby, let us in!"

Nothing. Just pounding.

"Stand back," I tell Linda, and I take a few steps run up and charge at the door.

It shakes, but does not open.

The pounding gets louder.

I try again, and this time I barge the door open, and knock a chair out of the way that had been wedged against it.

Bobby is at his window. Lifting his head back and striking it into the glass, then lifting his head back, striking it into the glass, lifting it back, striking it, back, strike, back, strike.

"Bobby, stop it!"

I run up to him, but just before I get there, his head

smashes through the glass, sending shards of glass flying throughout the room.

He turns and stares at us, blood streaming from an open wound in his forehead.

His eyes are vessels. His face is pale. His body stiff.

"Call 999," I tell Linda, who rushes from the room.

He picks up a loose shard of glass, holds it at arm's length, then plunges it into his eye, again and again

I grab his arm, but he turns the shard of glass toward me and swings it at my throat, and I throw myself backwards, duck just in time, releasing Bobby's arm.

Bobby turns to the window, leans forward, and topples out.

When the ambulance arrives, only one of us can go with him, so I let Linda go while I drive behind. We wait in the waiting room by intensive care, on the edge of the uncomfortable plastic seat, neither of us speaking.

A day later, when we return home without a son, the present is gone, and the house feels far emptier than it did before.

The Present continues later in the anthology...

CHRISTMAS WITH THE CANNIBALS

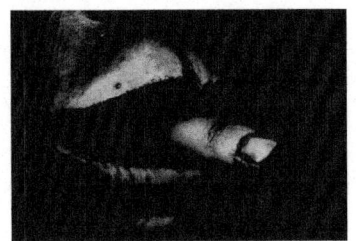

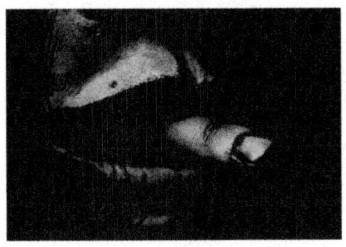

Oh, how I do delight at Christmas!

Mother and Father have made it ever so special for Archibald and me. Every year, we have an exquisite selection of gifts, curated from the finest establishments, and we open them with mirth and merriment.

Why, only this year, Mother and Father had their names emboldened on a plaque; *Cynthia and Bernard* engraved in gold and fastened to the wall above their grand poster bed.

They bought Archibald a framed football boot as worn by Harry Kane in the 2018 World Cup, signed by his favourite footballer and contained within crystal glass.

And for myself, they arranged for a star to be named Arabella, and had a man from the British Astronomical Society arrive on the eleventh hour of Christmas morning to present the picture of said star, along with a commemorative plaque certifying that my name is now attached to an exploded sun in space.

Of course, those were only the starter to our presents – the amuse bouche, if you will. Our mains are delivered shortly after by Graham, the butler with the strange moustache.

Then we delight in the anticipation of our Christmas feast. Mother cooks it, and it is the only time of the year she cooks as she does not wish for the staff to be involved in preparing the goose.

We sit around the table, salivating with enthusiasm for

what is to come. Mother brings in the vegetables first: deseeded aubergines, courgettes, crispy sprouts with bacon and garlic, and so forth.

But, as appetising as these appear, it is the goose we are waiting for. Of course, Mother knows how to put on a show, and she would not present the goose until last.

While we wait, we pull our crackers. Inside mine is a joke:

A well-dressed gentleman proceeded into a local drinking establishment. "Oh bother," he said.

With a giggle, I ask Archibald if he'll read out his.

"But of course," he says, and presents the small strip of paper before his eyes. "What did the bottle of Chateau 66 say to the Lambrini?"

"I don't know," I say. "What did the bottle of Chateau 66 say to the Lambrini?"

"Stop being so immature!"

Oh, how we chuckle heartily.

Then Mother appears in the doorway.

"Whatever is so humorous?" she asks.

"Mother, it's the joke, you must hear it," I say, prompting Archibald to turn toward her.

"What did the bottle of Chateau 66 say to the Lambrini?" Archibald says to Mother.

"Why, I do not know, what did the bottle of Chateau 66 say to the Lambrini?"

"Stop being so immature!"

The laughter resumes once more, all of us caught up in the hilarity. Mother chuckles so much she is almost reduced to tears.

"Oh, they get me every year," she says as she returns to the kitchen.

Also in my Christmas cracker is a gift. It appears to be a Cartier diamond necklace.

I suppose it will go with my other two.

"What did you get?" I ask Archibald.

He presents a set of keys, and reads the attached bit of cardboard.

"It says these keys are for a 2009 Eclipse yacht," he announces.

Oh, bother. I'd have loved that. I smile at him, but really, I'm a little disappointed.

The final item in the Christmas cracker is a hat. Well, it's more of a crown, really. It has a few gems on it, and appears to be made out of white gold. I don't particularly wish to wear it, but with everyone else wearing theirs, I do so. Don't want to be a bad sport on Christmas, do I?

"Are we ready for the goose?" Mother calls from the kitchen.

"Oh, yes!" I say.

"Rather!" Father concurs.

"Of course!" Archibald exclaims.

We hear the StanKraft Steel Trolley approaching the dining room, along with the smells and aromas that encapsulate Christmas so perfectly. And there it is, wheeled in by Mother; the goose. So eloquently positioned, its face at the front holding an apple, on all fours with its posterior in the air.

"Wow!" I say, and Archibald and Father both join in their wondrous excitement.

Mother places the goose by the table.

"Would you like to carve?" she asks Father.

"Of course!" he replies, and takes the knife, standing

over the goose. "Who would like rump, who would like thigh, and who would like something else?"

I try and decide what I would like, then notice Archibald. He looks perturbed, like he's about to cry, staring at the goose with a most unpleasant expression.

"What is it?" Mother asks.

"It keeps looking at me!"

"What does?"

"The goose, it keeps looking at me!"

I look at the goose's face and, sure enough, it is staring at Archibald. Then it turns to me.

"Oh, my," I say. "It's looking at me too."

It is most unsettling, I must say, to have one's meal stare at you before you eat it!

Then it tries making a noise. A moan, one that is stifled by the apple in its mouth.

"Did you cook it for long enough, my dear?" Father asks.

"I believe so," Mother replies. "Mostly, I drugged it so it would stay still while we ate."

"I really do not like it staring at me!" I say, and oh how this Christmas is not turning out like it should. "And how old is this goose, anyway?"

"Why, this one is a male at around thirty-three years old."

"There's hair on its armpits!"

"Yes, but I shaved the rest of its body, I promise."

It makes another sound, muffled by the apple, trying to say something like *help me*.

I stand, backing away, disliking this situation very much.

"Darling," Father says, staying ever so calmly, "is there a way we could stop it from staring at us?"

Mother looks at the goose's face. Its eyes wander to hers and she looks just as unsettled as we do.

"I suppose," she says, still thinking about it. "Well, I mean, we could gouge its eyes out."

Father turns to Archibald and myself.

"Would that be satisfactory?" he asks.

Archibald and I exchange a look.

"I think so," I say. "I suppose then it won't be able to look at us."

"The blood may spoil the meat around its face, but that's not always the best part anyway, is it?"

"I wasn't particularly excited by the face, Father. I think I was leaning more toward thigh."

"Well then, that's decided. Do you have the cooking fork to hand, dearest?"

Mother thinks for a moment, then rushes back into the kitchen. We glare at this most rude goose, that still stares at us all, then Mother re-enters the room moments later with the cooking fork.

Father takes it and stands in front of the goose with a hand on his chin, deep in thought. It makes more noise and stares wide-eyed up at him.

"I'm not sure what the best way is to go about this," he says.

I sigh. Really, I am hungry, and this needs to be done.

"May I, Father?" I say, just wishing the ordeal could be done with.

Father hands me the fork.

"Wait, I don't want you doing this!" Mother says.

She rushes into the kitchen and returns seconds later, presenting me my Risdon & Risdon original black apron.

"There," she says. "That's better."

Good point. I am wearing my favourite Dolce & Gabanna maroon frock and I do not wish for it to be painted in blood.

After putting the apron on, I stand before the goose, and decide which eye to go for first.

I believe the right one is the widest, the one that stares the hardest. I hold the cooking fork back, getting as much leverage as I can, then swing it forward, plunging it into the goose's eyeball. I hold it there, listening to it squelch, twisting it around and around, then retract the cooking fork, leaving a large pool of dark red blood pouring from its eye socket.

Father, Mother and Archibald applaud.

"Oh, very good, dear! Very good indeed!"

The other eye still stares at me, and the goose is making a lot of noise if I do say so myself. It's constant, and it's irritating.

I do my best to ignore it, plunge the cooking fork into the second eye, and twist it; but I did not expect that when I retracted the utensil I would be bringing the eyeball out with it!

I pull the cooking fork away, and the eyeball hangs down the goose's cheek by a something loose and red, swinging like the metronome my piano teacher uses.

The goose's noises become worse so, to make it stop, I remove the apple from its mouth and stick the cooking fork into its tongue.

By the time I return the apple to the goose's mouth, it makes no noise whatsoever, and appears to have gone quite limp.

"Oh dear," Father says. "I believe you killed it."

Disappointed faces stare back at me.

"Oh, I am so sorry," I say.

"It's a shame," Mother interjects. "It just means the meat will be rotten if we want to have it tomorrow."

I bow my head in disgrace.

Evidently witnessing my despair, Father adds, "Well we'll just have to eat it all today!"

My head lifts and we all smile and we're happy again!

And finally, we are able to sit down and have the grandest, most satisfying Christmas dinner yet. By the time we have finished the goose, we are, as the lesser educated among us may say – 'stuffed.'

Yet I still feel excitement when Mother says, "Who's ready for pudding?"

"Hurrah!" we all respond.

"Just wait until you see the Christmas pudding," she says.

Father follows her into the kitchen, ready to light it – as, of course, it is tradition to cover the pudding in brandy and set it on fire.

And, unlike the goose, when Mother brings in the Christmas pudding, it barely squirms.

It is the most delicious Christmas dinner yet.

ME AND MY CHRISTMAS JUMPER

1

I am delighted – no, more than delighted, I am thrilled – by our new vicar's service. He has a way with words, one that only a true servant of God can achieve. I feel myself on the edge of the pew, my hands clasped together, hanging on every word.

"And I will finish with a verse from Psalm 139:14," he says, and I am terribly sad that the service is coming to an end. "I thank you, God, for making me so mysteriously complex. Everything you do is marvellously breath-taking. It simply amazes me to think about it. How thoroughly you know me, Lord."

He closes his Bible and smiles at the small group of dedicated churchgoers spread across the benches.

"Remember, however much you lose sight of who you are, the Lord still knows. Oh – and please don't forget, our next service will be our Christmas Eve service. I hope to see you there."

I go to clap, but no one else does, so I just stare at him, astonished, as he walks to the altar, gently places two fingers in the water, and makes a cross over his body.

I want to talk to him, to thank him, I am desperate to – but that Theresa lady gets there first. I wait as they talk, and the other members of his congregation wait behind me.

"Vicar," I say when it's finally my turn. "That was so lovely!"

I grab his hand and shake it, placing my other hand on it. Covid regulations be damned – I must thank this man!

"Thank you ever so much, that was truly enlightening!"

"Thank you," he says, not really smiling, but still making eye contact.

"That was a lovely service, really lovely, I am so happy to have you as our vicar here."

"Well, I am pleased that you have welcomed me so well."

His eyes shift to the person behind me, and he tries to release his hand from mine, but I am not done yet.

"My name is Margaret," I tell him. "I live in the cottage on Handle Lane."

"Lovely," he says, and turns to speak to the lady behind me.

"Where were you before here? They must be missing you."

He forces a smile. "I am sure they are. Please, I have other people to attend to."

He goes to speak to that lady again, but I step in front of her.

"I will be attending on Christmas Eve," I tell him. "I am really looking forward to it."

He places a hand on my wrist and releases his hand from my grip.

"I am delighted," he says. "Now please, excuse me."

He walks away and speaks to a few other people. I don't leave quite yet – instead, I gaze, watching him interact, so pleased to have such a wonderful vicar for once.

Me and My Christmas Jumper

Eventually I leave, taking the short walk to my cottage. Tibbles rubs against me as I enter, and I give him a little fuss before making myself a cup of tea and watching my recording of *Question Time* from earlier this morning. They are debating whether young people are frustrated, and it puzzles me as, throughout the entire debate, I can't quite fathom what they are suggesting young people are frustrated about. I mean, it feels like the topic is incomplete.

When the time reaches six o'clock, I start preparing myself for work on Monday morning. I ready my beige skirt – ankle-length of course – along with a flowery blouse and a brown cardigan, and I place them on the dresser. One should always have your outfit ready the night before!

Then I suddenly remember I hadn't opened today's advent calendar – how could I be so silly?

I find door number twenty-one, and behind it is a chocolate in the shape of a piece of holly, with a picture of Mary on a camel behind it. I don't quite get what a piece of chocolate shaped like holly has to do with Mary on a camel, but I suppose many of these advent calendar manufacturers don't quite understand what they are doing. In fact, I had to do quite a lot of browsing online to find one with both chocolate and the nativity story, but I came across this wonderful site called Amazon. They sell all kinds of things there! Have you heard of it?

My Nokia phone makes a sound. How odd. Usually Mummy messages on a Saturday morning; I'm not used to receiving messages from other people.

I place my reading glasses on the end of my nose, lift the phone to the light, and read. It is Barry, my boss at work. He is saying that, since we have only two days left in work before Christmas, we are invited to wear Christmas jumpers.

Oh, how lovely! It is a shame in a way, as I was looking forward to wearing that cardigan, but a Christmas jumper will be jolly festive. Only problem is, it's late on a Sunday and I'm not sure which shop will be open.

Endeavouring to find one, I put on my large coat with the furry hood, buckle my shoes, and take my Hello Kitty bag into the street on a mission to find a festive jersey.

I hope it's woolly, so it's nice and warm.

2

It is dark and cold, and I don't like it. At this late hour of the evening, town is full of scary-looking people and youths wearing tracksuits even though they aren't exercising.

What's more, every shop is shut, and I have no idea where to go. *Marks & Spencer's* was my first try, then *Oxfam*, then the *Edinburgh Woollen Mill* – but nothing!

There is one shop, however, down an alley, that I notice has an open sign on the door. Its windowpane is painted black, and it doesn't even have a name. In the window, however, amongst large, black boots and leather jackets and hoodies with skulls on, is a fluffy jumper, blue and white and green, with a picture of Rudolph. Rudolph's nose even sticks out, like a little ball, and it looks rather endearing.

I take a deep breath and enter the shop. It's rather smelly, and very small. In fact, there is no room at all for social distancing, and I find myself having to hold my arms across my chest as I walk between the rails of clothes and the walls.

I reach the counter and find a man crouched down with his back to me, sorting something out on the floor.

"Excuse me?" I say.

He stands and turns toward me. He is small, with a few stray hairs combed over a balding head, and eyes that are wide and always staring.

"I would like to inquire about the Christmas jumper in the window," I say.

The man grins a rather large grin. It spreads across his face, much like the Grinch's smile does.

"By all means," he says, and his voice is a little chaotic.

I look forward to getting out of here.

He collects the jumper from the shop window and shows it to me. The brightness and happiness of the jumper is in such contrast to the rest of the shop that I find it very odd that they sell such a thing.

"How much is it to purchase?" I ask.

"For you," the man says, "twenty pounds."

It's a little steep for something I'm only going to wear for a few days, but it's unlikely I will find anywhere else able to sell me one now.

"Do you take Mastercard?"

"We do."

"Lovely. I would like to purchase this Christmas jumper with my Mastercard then."

I take out my card and await his machine, not wishing him to touch my card – in fact, I don't want any part of me or my possessions to touch anything in this shop other than the jumper.

I place my card on the reader, wait for the beep that signals a successful transaction, and take the jumper.

"Would you like a bag?" he asks.

Me and My Christmas Jumper

"No thank you, that would be quite all right. Thank you for providing me with your service."

"You're welcome."

I take the jumper and hurry out of the shop, out of the alleyway, and back to the high street where there are plenty of lamplights.

I hold the jumper out before me. It is a little large, but that's okay, it will be extra cosy.

I return home, place my jumper in my bag, and watch my recording of this morning's *Songs of Praise* before getting an early night. Today has been quite an ordeal!

3
***

I arrive at work early with my jumper in my bag, in time to have breakfast before we commence working activities, just as I do every morning. Barry is in his office, and as I walk past, he says, "Good morning."

"Good morning to you too," I reply, and make my way into the staff kitchen.

I take out a soft-boiled egg and use a knife to spread it across two slices of bread that I already buttered at home. I add some of the prawn mayonnaise I made on Saturday in there too, just for a treat, and place it into the microwave.

Eric, a colleague in his mid-twenties with patchy stubble on his chin, walks in and immediately grips his nose.

"What is that smell?" he says.

"I don't know."

He looks at the microwave. "Are you heating up egg and fish?"

"Actually it's prawns, which aren't technically fish, they are crustaceans."

"Fucking hell, Margaret, that's mank," he says, and leaves the room. I'm not quite sure what *mank* means, as I am not particularly well-versed in the youth's vernacular, so I go about my business unperturbed.

Once my cup of tea and sandwich are ready, I take them to my desk. Eric sits behind me, next to Sandy, a young lady in her late twenties who changes her hair colour a lot, and I sit next to Charlie, a man in his thirties who perspires through his Star Trek t-shirts quite profusely.

Eric mumbles something as I walk past, and the others snigger, and I wonder what he said that's so funny. They make noises too, similar to the one Eric made when he entered the kitchen, but again, I'm not quite sure what that is about.

I sit on my chair and hear more sniggering.

They must have been telling jokes or something. I like jokes, but not the ones they tell. They are far too crude for me. I much prefer the kind of jokes you find in a Christmas cracker, or the occasional limerick.

I switch on my computer and try to get comfortable, before noticing that my skirt is caught on something.

I stand, and my skirt is still attached to the chair. I pull it up, and it rips a little bit, leaving a bit of material attached to what looks like chewing gum.

"Oh my," I say, disappointed that my favourite skirt is damaged. "How did that get there?"

The others are all looking at me.

"I have no idea," says Eric, and they all snigger again. I wonder what was so funny about the joke he told.

Ah well, I'll have to get my sewing kit out tonight. I was planning on watching my DVD box set of *Downtown Abbey*, the one with the Christmas episode – but I suppose I can do both at the same time.

I check the back of my skirt. The hole is very small, probably unnoticeable, but there is a bit of gum stuck to it, so I make my way to the bathroom and use water and my thumbnail to scrape the remnants away.

When I come back, my sandwich is no longer on my table.

"Where on earth is my sandwich?" I say.

The others look blankly at each other.

"You must have eaten it," Eric says, still sniggering at that joke from earlier that really must have been mightily humorous.

"Ah well," I say, and sit down.

That's when I notice it in the bin. I don't remember putting it there, and I wonder how it happened.

4

The day proceeds as it normally does, though I keep feeling something on my back. Like someone is prodding me, but when I turn around, I see nothing. Eric is at his computer, and Sandy is looking at him and smiling but is too far away to have done it. And Charlie is next to me, so it can hardly be him as I'd notice.

Maybe it's a waft of wind or something. I don't know. I'm not quite sure, so I keep working.

The sniggering continues, though, and I am tempted to ask them to tell me the joke, but I decide against it. Their sense of humour is always so vulgar, I'm best not knowing.

After a few hours, Barry leaves his office and stands in front of all of us with his hands on his hips.

"Guys…" he says, with his warning tone of voice.

Oh dear. What's he annoyed about…

"Where are all the Christmas jumpers?" he says, then starts smiling.

Oh, he was pretending to be annoyed. The rascal!

He is right, though. Only Sandy is wearing her

Christmas jumper. It has a picture of Santa on it looking sad, and says *Bah Humbug*. It doesn't feel particularly festive.

I take mine out of my bag and put it on. It is so warm; I feel like I could wear it forever. I admire how Rudolph's nose sticks out again, and I do hope the others appreciate the humorous nature of my jumper, as it is worth quite the chuckle.

Charlie's jumper has Frosty the Snowman on it, and Frosty's tie sticks out of the jumper just like Rudolph's nose does on mine. I point at it and laugh, then indicate mine. How droll! We are both wearing jumpers with items sticking out in a comical way! Oh, this is going to be a humorous afternoon, I'm sure of it.

Eric's is a little more perplexing. It has Santa on it, and his arms are sticking to the side and disguising his head. The words *dabbing through the snow* are below Santa, and I am sure they are mistaken. Shouldn't it be *dancing through the snow*? That's quite a poor error to make, considering it's probably a mass-produced product. I wonder if all the jumpers of the same design have a similar spelling error.

Bizarrely, Sandy seems to find it quite funny. She even imitates the movement Santa is doing on the jumper. Maybe the error is intentional? If so, I don't see why, it's just not funny.

Anyway!

After we've had a good look at each other's lovely garments, we return to our computer screens. I have a few things to process and a few emails to reply to and, even though the prodding feeling on my back repeats every now and then, I manage to get most of my work done.

Then, out the corner of my eye, following the last prod, I see Eric move, and hear a little shuffle.

Did he tap me on the shoulder? Is it him that keeps prodding me, does he want something?

I turn around and address him.

"Is everything okay?"

"What?" he grunts, most impolitely.

"I asked if everything was okay? I thought you were tapping me, perhaps trying to gain my attention."

"No, not at all."

He looks at Sandy and they laugh. I don't get it.

"But I am sure you were poking me."

He grins. Turns to me. Sticks his finger out, prods my chest, and laughs again.

"Looks like I am now."

Sandy snorts she laughs so hard.

He goes to poke me again, but I grab his finger, wrapping my fist around it, and twist it upwards. I hear a click as it breaks, and Eric cries out in pain.

The whole time, I stare at Rudolph's nose sticking out of my jumper as it glows.

5

Barry asks me to sit in his office, so I do. You should always do what your boss tells you, especially if you want to be a good worker, so I wait on the comfy chair in the corner, next to the bookcase with the photograph of Barry and his wife. He looks a lot younger, and I wonder if he has no hair because he shaves it or because he lost it, because even in this picture he doesn't have any.

The commotion continues, and I watch – the walls of Barry's office are made of glass, so it's fairly easy to see. I'm not quite sure what's happening, but Eric is on the floor, clinging to his finger, whilst Sandy has a hand on his back. I think he's crying.

"It's broken, it's broken..." I hear him whimper.

I assume he's talking about his finger, seeing as that's what he's clutching. I do hope he's okay, that must be terribly painful.

Sandy and Eric leave, but Eric glances at me with the most disgruntled expression I've ever seen before they go. His nose is all furrowed and his eyebrows are low. It's not very becoming.

Once Barry has seen them off, he walks into the office and stands with his hands on his hips, staring at me. Am I supposed to say something?

"Sandy's taking him to hospital," Barry says. "I know they were being mean, but I never thought..."

He sighs, then sits next to me. He leans forward, clasping his hands together. He goes to speak, then doesn't, looking thoughtful.

Eventually, he does say something.

"What happened?" he says.

"Excuse me?"

"What happened, Margaret? Was it an accident? Or was it... intentional?"

"Was what intentional?"

"Eric's finger breaking."

"Oh my, it's actually broken?"

"Was it intentional, Margaret?"

"Well, I don't know, I suppose you'd need to ask him."

Another silence ensues where Barry stares at me. His expression is something between a scowl and sadness. I remember when I was little, Daddy used to have the same expression a lot when he spoke to Mummy.

"Really, I – I can't tell if you're trying to be funny, or trying to be difficult," he says.

"I am not doing either," I assure him. "I do not think it appropriate to be funny in the workplace, and I would not want to be difficult with someone who is in authority."

"Right. Okay. I see. Well... then.... I don't know, Margaret. Please help me to understand."

"Understand what?"

"What happened!"

"What happened when?"

"With Eric's finger."

"Gosh, I thought I already said – I really don't know. He's probably the best person to ask."

Barry stands. His hands grip into fists. He paces back and forth a few times.

"This is a serious situation," he says. "Eric could sue."

"Oh dear, could he?"

"Yes!"

"What would you do then?"

He stops pacing. Stares at me again.

"What would *I* do? Margaret, what is going on?"

"What is going on with what?"

"Stop it. Now. Just stop it – and explain. Please."

He looks at me like he's waiting for something. I feel like I'm being told off, and I look down, wondering what I should say.

That's when I notice – Rudolph's nose is glowing again!

I look up.

"Go fuck yourself you bald cunt."

"*What?*"

Rudolph's nose stops glowing. How on earth did it do that?

"Margaret, what did you just say?"

"I didn't say anything."

"Is this some kind of joke?"

"I assure you I do not joke in the office."

I am getting really confused. He is still staring at me, and I don't quite know what he wants me to say.

"Go home, Margaret. Think about this. And when you come back in tomorrow, perhaps have something better to say."

"Say about what?"

"Go!"

Me and My Christmas Jumper

Oh dear, he does seem mightily angry. Maybe it's best I do as he asks and go home. Perhaps he's granting me an afternoon off for all my hard work. In which case, he is a very kind man, and I acquiesce to his request quite eagerly, collecting my bag and making my way out of the office.

6

I'll be completely honest with you – this isn't the most pleasant walk home I've ever had. I don't mind the weather so much, as the grey skies and low temperatures are just part of the winter experience, and it wouldn't be Christmas without it. It's just this feeling, in my gut, following me around, about what happened to Eric.

I know I was there. I remember him poking me, and I remember being in Barry's office. What actually happened to him? How had he broken his finger?

It must have been awfully painful. And so close to Christmas, oh my...

I'm a positive person, yet with every person I pass, I see a little more evil. Like the man walking past me with the big coat and flat-cap who's staring at a woman across the road wearing the ear muffs and the short skirt in a very strange way; not a way that suggests he wants to take her to dinner!

A mother approaches me, and all I see is her grimace, and the way she pulls her child along by the arm. The boy appears to be slightly naughty, and is complaining about something, but the mother is not listening.

Eventually, she lets go of him and says, rather agitatedly, "Then walk home yourself!" and walks ahead.

The boy looks at me as he approaches, and I look at him.

Rudolph's nose starts glowing again, just as I hold my fist out and smack it into the boy's face and knock him into a puddle. I turn a corner a few minutes later and the nose isn't glowing anymore, but I cannot remember the last ten minutes of my walk.

I'm starting to wonder if there might be something off with this jumper. A ridiculous thought, really. It's just a jumper. Wool and warmth and a welcome smile from the most famous reindeer of them all.

Even so, I remove it, and place it in my workbag. I'm cold, but it only takes me another five minutes to arrive home.

I'm at a loss as to what to do, what with a whole afternoon free when I would normally be at work. In the end, I decide to watch a whole DVD box set of *Downtown Abbey*, ending with the Christmas episode. It is riveting, and I keep watching while I have my broccoli and cheese bake, my after-dinner cup of tea, and well into late evening. By the time it finishes, Tibbles is fast asleep on my lap. Just like him, I am awfully tired, and keen to leave the day behind.

I only have one more day in work before Christmas. One final day to spend with my delightful colleagues, and to be merry and jolly and full of cheer.

Yes, tomorrow is another day, and I am quite keen to get it started!

I go to bed, read two chapters of my Agatha Christie novel, and settle down to sleep just as it's getting good.

7

It has been the most awful day in work I have ever had.

I greeted Eric kindly when I entered, inquired about the health of his finger, and shared my hope that he was feeling better. He told me to, and I do not care to repeat this phrase too often, "Piss off," which shocked me to my very core.

I tried looking at Sandy to share a look, hoping she could explain his hostility, but she glared at me something fierce.

Even Charlie isn't willing to speak to me.

And yet it hasn't ended there.

Sandy and Eric are singing Christmas songs. Now, I have nothing against Christmas songs; in fact, I quite like them. On the way to Mummy's tomorrow I will be spending my train ride listening to The Rat Pack and Elvis Presley and all their Christmas albums. A good round of *Jingle Bells* does nothing but get me in the mood for merriment!

The lyrics of these songs, however... and I might be mistaken... seem to be different to the versions I know. And I am sure I catch my name, but can't be positive, as after all, why would they have rewritten famous Christmas jingles about me? It makes no sense!

Yet, during *Jingle Bells*, the second verse doesn't seem to repeat the first line, but is instead replaced with "Margaret smells."

Similarly, with *Ding Dong Merrily on High*, the second line sounded like "in heaven Margaret's bleeding."

I try and listen more carefully, but then they stop, and I suppose I must have heard wrong.

Every now and then, however, I hear my name, and it's followed by stifled giggles. I can't quite make out what's said, as they appear to just be random sentences.

That is, until I am listening carefully, waiting to decipher what is said, and I do hear, loud and clearly, the words they say:

"Margaret's a tight-ass bitch!"

I gasp.

They laugh. Oh, how they laugh.

But I have never heard something so...

I mean, the very nerve of...

Those words are...

I don't quite know what to say!

What is a tight-ass? To suggest there is anything tight about my buttocks is bizarre. But to imply that I'm a bitch is not very nice at all...

And they are still laughing.

"She's noticed!" Sandy whispers, quite indiscreetly.

I feel tears accumulating. This is horrible. Possibly the worst Christmas ever. Why would they be so cruel?

I rush to my feet and hurry to the toilets. As I leave, the laughter seems to grow, and that only makes it more horrible.

I lock the cubicle door, bury my face in my hands, and

oh how I cry! I cry so many tears I don't quite know how I have any water left in my body.

I take my handkerchief out of my sleeve and dab my eyes, but the tears just keep coming. I can't quite remember the last time I cried this much, but it must have been a long time ago.

Then my tears suddenly stop. My despair ceases, and my sorrow ends.

It's replaced by something else.

Something new.

I think it's anger. Bubbling beneath the surface. Rising up my body, coursing through my veins.

I am enraged. Fuming. Incensed.

And I have a feeling that I should put my Christmas jumper back on.

8

When I walk back into the office, Barry is leaning against the wall, and everyone is looking at me.

I avoid eye contact, not sure why they are staring, and go to my bag, pulling my jumper out, smiling at the familiar face of Rudolph.

"Margaret, Eric has something he'd like to say to you."

I don't look or pay attention. I just hold the jumper. Admire it. Feel it. There's something about it that grips me, that takes me over, that makes me feel like its willing servant.

"Sorry," Eric mumbles.

"Eric, I think you can do better than that."

"She broke my finger!"

"We discussed this – why did she break it?"

"Yes, I know."

"So try again."

Eric humphs and turns to me

"I am sorry, Margaret. For being mean to you. We shouldn't have, it was wrong, and I hope you forgive me."

I put the jumper on. Its power flows through me. Like I'm standing beneath a waterfall and streams of wrath are soaking my hair, cleansing my skin, and soaking me in its glory.

"Margaret?" Barry says.

I lift my head up, close my eyes, and pretend it's pouring on my face, drenching my hair.

"Margaret, did you hear what Eric said?"

I drop my head again. Turn to Eric. Grin.

"Do you accept his apology?" Barry asks.

Eric looks at me as well, but his face is different. He wears a limp smirk. He didn't mean a word of it.

"Well?"

"Oh," I say, my voice slow and dramatic. "Of course."

A rabid beast takes me over, like a hyena or a lion or a tiger, and I dive upon Eric, taking him and his chair to the ground.

I grab his stapler and, before anyone can take me off of him, I staple his face, not just once, but again, and again, and again and again, and again and again and again.

"Margaret!"

Barry's arms are around my shoulders and he's trying to pull me off, but he's too weak, he can't manage, and even Charlie can't help either.

I stuff the stapler down Eric's throat, swipe my long, sharp nails across his neck, then allow them to pull me off. I roll across the floor, away from their grasp, and land at Sandy's feet.

She's wearing a dress. A short dress. She always wears such short dresses. They are completely inappropriate for work. She doesn't even wear tights. She is a disgusting hussy, and I show her what a disgusting hussy she is by ripping her computer mouse from the desktop and shoving it up her skirt until she screams.

"You see, Sandy? You see how easy access it is? You see why it makes you such a slut?"

I jam the mouse higher and she screams harder and blood is dribbling down my arm so I lick it. I lick it off. All of it. Until my mouth is covered in blood the way a baby's is covered in food after dinner.

By the time just the USB wire dangles by her inner thighs she has passed out, and she is no fun anymore.

I notice Charlie on the floor with me, trying to pull me off Sandy.

He has two computer monitors on his desk. Large ones, too. They are always in the way of my computer. I don't understand why he needs so many screens. So I hit them, and the first falls off the table and the screen smashes when it impacts his skull. I grab the second, lift it above my head, and when his feeble arms manage to push the first screen off of his dizzy body, I am able to plunge the second downwards.

I turn to Barry.

He is on the floor. A few feet away. Staring at me. Crawling backwards.

He looks so afraid.

Silly Barry.

He runs and I sprint toward him on all fours. He isn't fast enough and I dive upon his back, take him to the ground, and sink my teeth into the fleshy side of his neck, sinking them harder and harder, deeper and deeper

Once he stops moving, I move away, lean against the wall, and dial 999.

I look down at Rudolph's nose.

It isn't glowing.
How strange.

9

I sit in the back of the police car, nothing but the flashing lights of other police cars illuminating the darkness.

My arms are handcuffed behind my back, but don't need to be. I'm not going anywhere.

People stand outside the car window, taking photos of me. Some with phones, some with cameras. I give them a smile then turn away.

That's enough voyeurism for today, you nosy vultures.

I catch sight of myself in the rear-view mirror. My face is a mask of blood. If you didn't know me before today, you wouldn't even be able to tell my ethnicity. Though I do like what it's done to my hair. It was grey, now it's dark red colour. It's stylistic. I can see why Sandy changes her hair colour so much.

I look down at my jumper. Rudolph is also covered in blood, with splatters across his face and antlers, but he won't mind.

This is what he wanted, after all. This is what they don't tell you about in the songs.

Maybe they will, after today.

Maybe they'll make a Christmas song about me.

Frosty came alive on Christmas and was given a song, so why shouldn't I?

If Rudolph's courageous actions can be immortalised in verse, then why can't mine?

I smile at the jumper. At Rudolph. At his glowing nose.

And I thank him.

"Thank you," I whisper. "For finally giving me the courage to stand up for myself. I am forever grateful."

I think it's going to be a merry Christmas this year.

A very merry Christmas indeed.

CAROLLING WITH KILLERS

Hi there, and welcome to my second Christmas horror anthology. I am delighted to have you along for volume two!

I just thought I'd tell you about some of the research I have done for this anthology. Research for the first anthology was quite enlightening, but I was aware that the stories were very much subject to commercial traditions of Christmas, and I wanted to get a sense of other ways to celebrate the holiday. Therefore, it was my pleasure to be able to go carolling with a group of convicts, allowing me to experience an alternative Christmas, as well as meet some delightful people.

Bubba, especially, was an enlightening chap to spend time with. He'd been arrested and charged for murdering his ex-wife with a sledgehammer. He said he was innocent, so I took him at face value – after all, DNA evidence, an admission of guilt at the time, and CCTV footage of him executing the murder doesn't matter when a man is giving you his word.

Similarly, I met a fella called Mr Manson before he passed away a few years ago. He had the Hinduism symbol for prosperity and good luck tattooed upon his forehead. Many people told me it meant something else, but a google image search did in fact show that this was an accurate portrayal of the symbol, and I'm not quite sure what they were talking about.

I also met Johanna, who insisted that the attempted

murder of her prison officers was a complete misunderstanding. She was in fact pouring the kettle of hot water on the floor as a science experiment at the unfortunate moment that the prison officer stepped into her cell. She also explained that she was not punching him, but trying to help him up; her fists were just curling because they were cold, and she kept slipping on the water, which meant she accidentally caught him on the face once or twice or thirty-six times as the report suggested.

If I am to be honest with you, I barely survived the ordeal, as they handcuffed me to a pew and threatened me with a chainsaw – but when I expressed my sincere enthusiasm to go carolling with them the next day, they seemed pleasantly surprised, and were kind enough to let me go.

And so, to share with you the delight I had with these brilliant individuals on this cold, wondrous night, I wish to share with you the arrangements for some of the songs that we sang in case you wish to use them on your own carolling exploits. My particular favourite was *Good King Wenceslas is a Fucking Rat*, for which Bubba did a falsetto part that really made me quite emotional.

I hope you enjoy it, and perhaps we will see you one evening, when we knock on your door. Please, should this happen, do not be intimidated. Gunther may have the words *FUCK* and *CUNT* tattooed to his knuckles, but this is only because they said that *KITTEN* was too big to fit.

Also, I would advise you not to look Bulldog in the eyes. Mostly because he only has one, and he doesn't like it when people stare.

God bless the season and, as my new friends would say, tell anyone about this and I'll break your knees.

Season's greetings.

AWAY IN A MANGER BECAUSE JESUS AIN'T NO GRASS

Away in a manger
No crib for a bed
And if you snitch about it,
You'll end up dead.

The stars in the bright sky
Looked down where He lay
And the little Lord Jesus
Knows what he shouldn't say.

The cattle are sleeping
The Baby awakes
But little Lord Jesus
No grassing He makes.

I love You, Lord Jesus
Look down from the sky
And tell all my enemies
That they're going to die.

Be near me, Lord Jesus
I ask You to stay
Because anyone who talks,
Can't do nothin' but pray

Bless all the dear children
In Your tender care
And fit us for Heaven

Because that's where you'll end up if you say a fucking word.

SILENT ROBBERY TONIGHT

Silent night, holy night
The alarm is going, but it's all right,
Because we can hide behind this mother and child,
This Holy infant so tender and mild
And hide in heavenly peace
Hide in heavenly peace.

Silent night, holy night!
The coppers quake at the sight!
Glorious smashed windows from the bank afar;
Beaten security moan ow-we-oo-ah!
Christ the Saviour is born!
Christ, we best wait here til morn!
Christ, my balaclava is torn!

Silent night, holy night
Oh dear God, they've caught us all right,
Radiant blood from Thy holy face,
A stinging nose as we get out of this place,
Jesus, give us our worth,
Jesus, let us escape to our turf,
Jesus, Lord at Thy birth.

WE WISH YOU A MERRY BATTERING

We wish you a merry Christmas
We wish you a merry Christmas
We wish you a merry Christmas 'cause you won't
   see New Year

Good tidings we bring to you and your kin
We wish them a merry Christmas 'cause you
   won't see New Year

Oh, we'll make you into figgy pudding
Oh, we'll batter you into figgy pudding
Oh, I've never actually had figgy pudding
So bring some right here.
Good tidings we bring to you and your kin
We wish you a merry Christmas 'cause you won't
   see New Year

We won't go, do you want some?
We won't go, do you want some?
We won't go, do you want some?
Well bring it right here.
Good tidings we bring to you and your kin
We wish you a merry Christmas 'cause you won't
   see New Year

JOY TO THE WORLD

Joy to the world, that bitch is dead,
I decapitated her head,

It was the most beautiful scene,
When I removed and ate her spleen,
Removed and ate her spleen,
And removed, and removed, and ate her spleen.

Joy to the world, I heard her cries,
When I looked at her insides,
It only took me twenty mins,
To remove and eat her intestines,
Remove and eat her intestines,
Remove and eat, remove and eat, her intestines

Joy to the world, we sing forth,
Let the Earth receive her corpse,
Joy to the world, now we sing
Let all her screams ring.

THE PRESENT: SECOND CHRISTMAS

WE SPEND CHRISTMAS DAY AT BOBBY'S GRAVE, hardly able to believe it's been a whole year without him.

To have a son, then to have him taken from you, is the cruellest of fates, and Linda and I have barely survived it.

I took to silence. I remained cold and empty, said little to anybody, and avoided eye contact with those who tried to help.

Linda wasn't quite so willing to empty herself of emotions and, if anything, showed enough pain for both of us. At Easter, I found her in the bathroom having slashed her wrists. At Halloween, I found her outside screaming at a kid dressed up as The Grim Reaper, repeatedly shouting, "Why did you take him from me?" And, on Bobby's birthday in November, I found her wandering through his old primary school, asking his friends why they hadn't come to his party.

It's been tough but, on our wedding day, all those years ago, I vowed to stay in sickness and in health. This is her sickness, and we will face it together.

For me, the realities of this Christmas really hit home when I was in the toy store, and I found a present that Bobby would like, and I went to buy it, then I thought – *why am I in a toy store?*

I was starting the Christmas preparations without realising it, gathering the gifts to place under the tree and around the room, ready to wrap up and watch Bobby open on Christmas Day.

And so, on this cold, grey Christmas morning, we do not place presents out for our son – instead, we take a walk along the stream that leads us from our house to the cemetery, and we visit his grave.

I don't let myself cry. I keep my face vacant. I have to be strong for Linda, because once she begins crying, she does not stop. People walking by turn to look as her wails grow louder, then quickly turn away to avoid making eye contact. It's easier to just walk on and pretend you haven't seen it than to show interest or pretend to care.

I put my arms around her and she falls to her knees. I go to my knees with her, and I keep my arms there for as long as she needs them. If she feels like she has to spend the whole day knelt here in the cold, then that is what we will do. However long she needs to stay, whatever she needs, I will support her.

I bow my head and close my eyes. I can't bring myself to read the gravestone anymore. I chose those words a year ago, and I know them well enough. I just listen to my wife crying, let her sobs be the soundtrack to my despair.

Eventually, they stop. I keep my eyes closed and my arms around her. It takes a little while until I realise she's gone completely stiff.

I open my eyes and look at her. Her body is barely moving. If it weren't for the shivering of her arms, I wouldn't know she was alive.

But even though her face is empty, and her eyes are wide; they are fixated on something.

"Linda?" I say.

She doesn't react.

"Linda, what is it?"

Nothing. Just stares. Determined stares.

I turn to look at what she's staring at, and I don't believe it at first. It's not possible. My eyes are deceiving me, I'm seeing things, this is what trauma does – it creates images; your mind conjures them up.

But Linda seems to see it too.

Red and gold wrapping paper. A large box. Across the graveyard.

Linda stands.

"Linda? What are you doing?"

She walks forward robotically, her muscles stiff.

"Linda, don't."

I don't know how a present can do this to someone, but I know I can't lose her too.

"Stop!"

I rush after her, trying to pull her back, but somehow she's too strong. I even put my arms around her and pull her away, but she wriggles out of my grasp and strides forward.

She reaches the present. Covers it in her shadow.

"Please, Linda, don't," I say, at her side, still trying to pull her away, but she doesn't pay me the slightest bit of attention.

She's changed, just like Bobby did. Gripped by something, taken over, uncompromising in her determination to discover what is inside the present.

"Linda, please–"

She turns and punches me, her fist into my jaw, and it knocks me to the ground. It takes a moment for me to gather myself, to push myself to my knees.

When I look up, she's already lifted the lid of the present and is staring inside.

She closes the lid and looks back at me.

Linda's not there. Whatever is behind those eyes, it's not the woman I love.

It's something else.

She walks away from the present, out of the cemetery, toward the stream.

"No!" I shout, and I run after her, grab her, but she pushes me off.

I try harder, grabbing her arm, grabbing her body, pulling her back, but she has gained strength I can't falter, and I can do nothing.

She reaches the stream and punches me in the gut.

I fall to my knees as she lowers herself to hers.

She stares at her reflection in the waves of the water, then submerges her entire head beneath the surface.

"No, Linda!"

I try to pull her out, reaching into the water and grabbing her head, pulling and pulling, but she is too strong. It's like something is pushing her head under and I can't match its strength.

With a heave and a growl I pull harder, and harder still, and I manage to take her out of the water.

When she looks at me her pupils are gone. She retracts her fist then punches me, and everything goes dark.

When I awake, I have no idea how long I've been knocked out. I rub my eyes, lean up, and look for Linda.

Her body lies limply on the pavement, her head in the water.

I pull her out, but I already know she's dead.

A few people walking past run over, and one of them tries CPR. I know it won't work, but I let them try.

I hear someone on the phone, asking for an ambulance, but it feels distant, somewhere in the background. Someone tries to talk to me, but I can't hear them, I am too busy looking over my shoulder at the graveyard, wondering what it is she saw, wanting to know what it is that's taken my family from me.

The present is already gone.

The Present continues later in the anthology...

CHRISTMAS NIGHT OF THE LIVING DEAD

1

BILL DECIDED SOMETHING, and it was something he had been considering for a while: *Christmas is boring as fuck.*

All this excitement, anticipation, enthusiasm, and for what? Dry turkey, a pair of socks from Grandma, and a day forced to spend with the family.

When he was six, yeah, it was good. He believed in Santa and he spent a whole day playing with toys. Now, at fifteen, he received the zombie game he'd been waiting months to receive, then told he couldn't even play it as he had to spend time with Grandma.

Unfortunately, *spending time* also meant *sitting silently in the same room.*

She was old. It wasn't her fault, and Bill did not blame her for it, but it did mean that there was little he could do with her. Normally, she just sat on the comfiest armchair of the living room, staring straight ahead, with her white bushy hair and her veiny arms and her spindly fingers barely moving.

When he was a kid, Grandma would spend all

Christmas Day playing with him. Whatever toy he had, Grandma would get on her knees and join in. He used to look forward to it. Now, however, she was as lifeless as a cucumber.

Bill sighed and slumped down on the sofa, staring at *Zombie Rage Rampage III* in his hands, the game that *Zombie Magazine* rated five stars and *Computer Games Forever* rated as one of the best zombie games ever made, knowing he was going to have to wait until Boxing Day to play it.

He sighed again. A big huff. Turned to Grandma. Considered making conversation.

But what would he say?

"So you been up to much lately?" he tried.

Her absent stare did not break, and her arms did not flinch.

"Fuck a duck," he muttered, sliding so far down the sofa he almost fell off. Normally, he would not dare use such language in front of his family. But Grandma didn't care. How could she care when she wasn't even aware?

Bill drummed his fingers on his belly. Picked a loose bit of fur off his *The Walking Dead* t-shirt. Wiped his nose. Straightened his genitals.

His gaze drifted across the room, past the photos of his parent's wedding day, past the baby photos of himself, past various ornaments, and to the window – where something drew his attention.

He stood. Edged toward the window. Wiped the condensation off the glass, and gazed through the snowy landscape. On the field beside his house, close enough to see but far enough away to be difficult to make out, there were two people on the ground.

What on earth were they doing?

He looked back at Grandma, hoping to exchange a look, then wondered why he bothered.

He squinted, staring into the distance, but still unable to tell what was going on.

He collected his phone from the arm of the sofa, placed it against the window, and opened the camera App. He zoomed and waited for the image to focus.

A woman was lying on the ground. She wasn't moving.

A man was leaning over her.

What was the guy doing?

Hang on...

No, he couldn't be...

"Holy turkey balls..."

Bill knew what this guy was doing. Oh, he knew all right.

The man was feeding! He had blood around his jaw and intestines in his hand, shovelling them into his mouth like Bill's fat cousin does with pigs in blankets.

Then the man looked up, staring straight at him.

Bill couldn't believe it.

Never mind the game...

This year, he was going to be fighting zombies for real!

Happy bloody Christmas to me!

2

BILL DIDN'T WASTE ANY TIME. He rushed into the kitchen, searching for a weapon, finding a kitchen knife, then changing his mind.

A knife was too small. A zombie would have to get too close for him to use it. He had a cricket bat in the garage, he'd use that!

"What are you doing?" his mum asked.

Bill had barely acknowledged she was there.

"I have to go do something."

"Do what?"

"Outside, there's... just something. I have to go deal with it."

"What about Grandma?"

"She'll be fine."

"You are not leaving your Grandma alone, Bill!"

"But, Mum–"

"That's final! Whatever you are doing, you take her with you."

And so, with Grandma in tow, he endeavoured to leave the house – leaving the house with Grandma, however, was not a simple thing. All the momentum he'd gathered and energy he'd accumulated and adrenaline that had flowed through him, preparing him to go kill some zombies, went.

Because first he had to get Grandma ready.

He collected her wheelchair from the downstairs cupboard. He started unfolding it, and caught his finger in the process.

"Dammit," he said, looking at his finger and expecting a bruise, to find it was dribbling blood.

He went to the kitchen and found a plaster from the drawer. After holding a kitchen towel over the cut and waiting for the bleeding to subside, he finally placed a plaster over it.

He checked the time. Ten minutes had passed, that was all. He tried to stay invigorated.

He resumed opening the wheelchair, which proved more difficult than he'd anticipated. It was a fiddly contraption, and he kept opening it the wrong way. In the end he had to ask his mum for help.

"I'm busy cooking dinner, go find your dad," she said.

Bill searched the study, the bedroom, all of upstairs, and even knocked on the toilets. Finally, he found his dad in the garden, sitting on a bench.

Why on earth was he sitting out in the cold? *No time to ask.* Dad didn't really do short answers, and Bill didn't have time for a long-winded explanation, so he asked for help with the wheelchair, and Dad clicked it into place a little too easily.

Bill checked the time. Fifteen minutes. *Come on, let's go.*

He returned to Grandma. Placed the wheelchair next to her. Lifted her into it, finding her to be surprisingly light.

He collected her coat, put one of her arms through the

sleeve, then the other, and zipped it up, adding her gloves to her hands and her shoes to her feet.

Then, just as he was about to leave, her catheter became loose, and a bag half full of urine slipped off her leg. He tried to place it back by her leg, but it wouldn't stick.

He left the room, searching for duct tape, expecting there to be some in the toolbox in the cupboard under the stairs. Unfortunately not.

He sought Dad out again, who said he had some in the study. He walked, slowly and purposeless, through the house and collected it for him.

Half an hour. *Still ready! Still buzzing!*

Bill took the duct tape, taped the bag to Grandma's leg, placed the duct tape at the bottom of the wheelchair, and wheeled her through to the front door.

"Dinner's ready!" called Mum.

For fuck's sake...

3

A LARGE, LAVISH CHRISTMAS DINNER was had by all. Bill's dad fed Grandma a few mouthfuls, and she even swallowed a few. Everyone heaped praise upon Bill's mum for the good work, and she blushed in response.

Once the dinner and the Christmas pudding were eaten, Bill leapt from the table and said he was popping out. His dad swiftly reminded him to take Grandma.

"Take care of her!" he said. "I expect my mum back in one piece!"

And so, whilst wheeling Grandma's wheelchair and holding a cricket bat under his arm, Bill made it to the field to find the woman's corpse on its own, and the man he'd seen feeding on her was gone.

Her chest was open, and her insides were missing. This would make most people gag, but Bill had played so many zombie games that he was now immune to such a sight.

He put the brakes on Grandma's wheelchair, took the cricket bat, and looked around.

A fog hovered over the snowy landscape. There was an absence of life, with most people at home enjoying their Christmases with each other. Aside from a dog walker in the distance, Bill could see no other movement, from the living or the undead.

Then the woman by his feet shifted a little. At first, Bill assumed a rat had found its way inside her body, or she was releasing gas as dead bodies often do.

Then the woman groaned. Her head turned, and her red, bloodshot eyes locked on Bill's.

Yes! he thought. *This is it!*

The woman pushed herself to her feet, a few loose guts tumbling out of her otherwise empty torso, and stood upright. She struggled to move, what with her chest being open and all that, but managed to stagger toward Bill with her arms out.

This was it. This was the moment Bill had fantasised about.

An actual zombie apocalypse!

He would kick arse in this scenario, he knew it.

He knew all the best ways to survive a zombie outbreak:

- Do not use a gun as weapon, it can run out of ammo. Use a handheld weapon.
- Use height if you need to – zombies will not be able to climb a ladder to get to you.
- Endurance, endurance, endurance. Running will help you get away, especially if these are the slow kind of zombies.
- Be ready for violence. Blood and gore isn't pretty!
- Water is your friend. They can't cross rivers.

And, after sizing up the slow-moving attacker limping toward him, he concluded for sure that these were slow zombies. They weren't *World War Z* or *28 Days Later* zombies; they were *Night of the Living Dead* and *The Walking Dead* zombies.

Which aren't that scary, to be honest, once you get over the vile sight of them. In fact, they would only incite fear if they were in huge numbers.

As it was, this was one-on-one.

With a scream, Bill charged forward, his cricket bat in the air and, just as the woman ran her cold, hard fingers over his chin, he swung the bat into her head, hard, knocking her to the ground.

She did not get up again.

Bill felt a sense of pride. This was turning out to be a good Christmas after all!

He turned to Grandma. Smiled at her.

"You doing all right?" he asked.

She didn't reply. Of course she didn't. But he felt invigorated, revitalised, full of energy, and he didn't mind. She had been wonderful when he was younger, but now it was her turn to be taken care of.

A groan alerted him, and he quickly turned around.

There were four of them approaching. An old man, an old woman, a middle-aged man, and a boy. It looked like a family. Perhaps a zombie had found its way into their home, and this family hadn't survived.

Well, Bill best put them out of their misery.

He ran forward and swung the bat at the old man. Despite being old, he was still quite muscular, and Bill knew it was best to kill the biggest threat first.

The old man's teeth flew out of his mouth, landing at the

end of a splatter of blood, and he fell to the ground, limp and lifeless.

The boy was at Bill's back, reaching out for him, so Bill knocked him away with the end of the handle. It wasn't enough to kill the zombie, but it was enough to throw him temporarily off balance while Bill dealt with the bigger threats.

He turned to the old woman and the middle-aged man. She had blood crusted to her cheeks, and a loose bit of skin stuck between her teeth, while his chest was cut open and a long piece of intestine trailed on the floor. He kept almost tripping up on it, desperately moving toward Bill whilst his innards dangled between his legs.

Bill kicked the middle-aged man back, and he tripped and fell over his loose body parts, leaving Bill with the opportunity to turn to the old woman and upper cut her with the bat.

Her chin dislocated, but it wasn't enough, so Bill struck her with the bat in her nose, smashing it across her face and knocking her to the floor.

He dove upon the middle-aged man, lifted the cricket bat high, and plunged it downwards upon the man's face, twice, then three times.

He stood, looking for the kid.

Where was he?

Bill looked around, back and forth, trying to see where the boy had gone.

He wiped some blood from his eyes. He wasn't sure which of the zombie's blood it was, but he had to be careful – he couldn't let any in his mouth. He didn't know for sure how these zombies infected people, but he didn't want to risk letting any blood mix with his saliva for fear that may turn him into one.

He continued to look, persistently searching for the boy.
Then Bill saw him.
Sitting on Grandma's lap.
Sinking his teeth into her throat.

4

"No!" Bill cried out. "Grandma!"

He sprinted toward her and thwacked his cricket bat into the child's chest, sending him flying across the air and skidding along the snow.

Bill didn't look at Grandma. Not yet.

He couldn't bare it.

First, he dealt with the little scrote.

The boy leapt to his feet, quicker than his elders were able, still with youthful energy even while dead. His teeth dripped with blood, his clothes marked with the remnants of those he'd already killed, and his fingers curved like claws, ready to dig his fingernails into any opponent who took him on.

The boy charged at Bill, but all Bill needed to do was lift the cricket bat to head height and let the child run into it.

Half of the boy's face shattered, his skull collapsing in on itself, and he lay in the snow. His leg twitched for a moment, and Bill watched until he was confident the zomboy wouldn't be getting up.

He turned slightly, glancing over his shoulder, not wanting to look, but knowing he must.

So he turned. But he kept his eyes closed.

Then he opened them.

Grandma sat limply; even more limp than she did before. A large chunk of flesh had been taken out the base of her throat.

But she could still be okay, right?

She could still live?

After all, Bill didn't know whether a bite was enough to change someone into a zombie.

He dropped his head. This was denial. He knew, deep down, in his gut, that her long life had come to an end, and something else would take over soon.

So he began preparations, ready for the moment she changed.

He retrieved the duct tape from the bottom of the wheelchair and, trying not to look at her gaping wound, he wrapped it around her arm, fastening it to the arm of the wheelchair, then did the same with the other.

Then he did the same with her legs. Fastening one to the wheelchair, then the other.

Of course, those zombie experts among you will be screaming at Bill right now, telling him he should kill her, that you can't let your emotions cloud your judgement, that she's already gone; that it's no good.

But it's not *your* grandma.

For the final touch, Bill lifted the collar of her cardigan and covered the wound. It was low enough down that it could be easily concealed, and one would never know what happened to her.

And he waited.

Standing before her, watching her, anticipating the moment, getting colder as the wind became stronger.

He wasn't sure how long he waited, but eventually, it happened.

The legs twitched first. A quick spasm in one, then the other.

Her arms joined in next.

Then a long, exasperated groan escaped her dry, cracked lips, and she lifted her head, focussing her gaze on Bill.

She tried to get up, tried to push herself forward, reaching open-mouthed for Bill. But she was restrained well enough that she was unable to move.

She tried again, and again, and again, her sharp teeth leading the rest of her body.

When Bill was satisfied that she could not get to him, he took the handles of the wheelchair and began pushing.

"Come on, Grandma," he said. "Let's get you home."

5

"WHY WHEREVER HAVE YOU BEEN?" Bill's dad asked as soon as he walked through the door. "We've been waiting to play Charades!"

"Sorry, Dad, we were busy."

"Not getting in trouble, I hope."

"No, just going for a walk."

Then Dad turned to Grandma, bending down and smiling at her.

"And how are you, Mum?" he asked.

Bill watched, waiting for the moment Dad would realise; wondering what his punishment would be. He'd probably be grounded for months, have his Xbox taken away, never be able to play his zombie games again, forced to endure the rest of his adolescence in isolation.

Grandma snapped at Dad, her teeth chattering, reaching forward, trying desperately to taste his flesh.

Dad stood. Looked at Bill.

"Well, I don't know what you did to her," Dad said, and Bill prepared himself, made himself ready for the barrage of abuse he was about to receive.

Then Dad said, "But she seems the spriteliest she's been in a long time!"

Bill flinched, ready for the anger, then paused.

Wait, what?

"I mean, look at her," Dad said. "She's trying to get to me. She's barely moved for years, and now she can barely stop wriggling! What a dream!"

Bill nodded.

Yeah, Dad. Sure. It's a dream.

A bloody good dream.

"You should take her for walks more often," he told Bill, then walked into the living room, adding, "come on, game's about to start."

Bill wheeled Grandma in, put her in the corner, and they played.

Everyone remarked about how much Grandma did not stop wriggling, how she kept opening her mouth like she was hungry, how she was so full of energy, unlike the dormant old wretch they were used to. So much so, in fact, that when they went to bed, she didn't even sleep. And, on Boxing Day, she had more meat for lunch than everyone else put together.

And oh, how the family were thrilled! Such a drastic change, and such a wonderful one. Now everyone wanted to sit with her, and Bill was not subjected to consecutive Christmas Days sitting next to her in silence.

And that terminal illness she had? Well, she survived a great many years longer than the doctors had foretold... They declared it a phenomenon. In fact, the word they used was stupendous.

And, so long as Bill kept subtly feeding her pieces of flesh, no one knew, and she even ended up outliving them all.

It truly was a Christmas miracle.

INTERVIEW WITH KRAMPUS NOVEMBER 2020

10TH NOVEMBER 2020

In the corner of a café in Gloucester, I met the legend himself. He approached me with a grimace, and did not take my hand when I offered it – but was nevertheless eager to talk.

RICK
Well, I guess I should welcome you to my Christmas horror anthology for 2020.

KRAMPUS
Thank you, Rick, it's lovely to be here.

RICK
I was really pleased to have the opportunity to interview you for my book, I imagine it will be really interesting for my readers.

KRAMPUS
I am pleased I can educate people as to what I'm about. I'm an admirer of your books, too.

RICK
Oh yeah?

KRAMPUS
Oh, of course, *Psycho Bitches* really appealed to my love of violence.

RICK
That's wonderful. Now, I am familiar with your work, but for those who aren't, are you able to tell us a bit about yourself?

KRAMPUS
Ah, yes, of course. Well, I am basically the anti-Santa Claus, if you will. I oppose everything he stands for.

RICK
So peace and good-will to all men?

KRAMPUS
I'm not so much bothered about the peace, that's where many people are mistaken. Really, it's more the focus on presents; I generally like to torment people who forget what the essence of Christmas is about.

RICK
And what is the essence of Christmas about?

KRAMPUS
That's a very good question, Rick, thank you for asking it. For many people, it's family and hope and love. Of course, for me, it's murder and destruction.

RICK
Murder and destruction?

KRAMPUS
Yes, though, I mean, not exclusively. I also like mayhem, anarchy and genocide, but those are more like hobbies. For me, murder and destruction are more my job role. My purpose, if you will. Where I really excel in my work.

RICK
Well, it's good to still have interests outside of work.

KRAMPUS
Oh, gosh, yes, and it's so important, Rick, it really is. Sometimes I can get so focused on who I'm going to maim this year that it's good to be able to take a break. Get away from all the screaming and that. Sometimes even read a book.

RICK
Oh, really? Are you into reading?

KRAMPUS
Quite.

RICK
What are you reading at the moment?

KRAMPUS
Mein Kampf. It's riveting.

RICK
I see. Well, this is also a good opportunity to confront a few myths about you, if I'm able. For example, Wikipedia describes you as a horned, anthropomorphic figure described as half-goat, half-demon. Would you say this is accurate?

KRAMPUS
Well yes, fairly, actually. My mother was a goat, she grew up on a farm in Texas, and my father was the son of Beelzebub, one of the rulers of Hell.

RICK
What a pair! How did they meet?

KRAMPUS
Well, I think it was more of a fling than a relationship, as I was mainly brought up by my mum, but I always wanted to know more about my father and where I came from. When the time was right, she decided to introduce me to him.

RICK
And how was that?

KRAMPUS
Oh, just wonderful. Truly wonderful. He showed me how to burn someone alive without killing them to prolong the torture, he shared with me how to impale someone in a perfect way so as to keep their intestines apart from their liver and kidneys – oh, and he also showed me how to make a snowman.

                        RICK
    Sounds like that was a real turning point for you.

                       KRAMPUS
    I think that's definitely where I found my passion, yes, and
                    what led me to my work.

                         RICK
    Wikipedia says that you are from European folklore, yet you
              say your mother was from Texas?

                       KRAMPUS
    Yes, but she moved to Slovenia when I was very young. I
                 don't remember America.

                         RICK
    Yet there was actually an American movie made about you
                        in 2015.

                       KRAMPUS
                      (*Chuckles.*)
                    Yes, yes there was.

                         RICK
                    You seem amused?

                       KRAMPUS
    Well, Rick, honestly, I was a little bit amused when I saw it. I
    mean, they didn't ask to consult with me, there was no
    outreach from them, they basically did a movie about me,
    cast me as the villain, and didn't bother to talk to me. I was
    almost tempted to sue for libel, but was worried about what
                 that may do for my reputation.

RICK
Your reputation?

KRAMPUS
Well, yes – people fear me for my murderous side. If people then started fearing me because they were worried I would sue them, it wouldn't really help my image as a killer.

RICK
I thought the movie portrayed you well as a killer though.

KRAMPUS
No, yes, that's one part they touched on that I was on board with, only problem was... it was too tame. I mean, when I have a victim, I really like to get into them, tear them apart, see what their insides are like, you know? I don't mess around with stomping on vans, or with those killer gingerbread men. My father taught me to test someone's pain threshold early, see what I could get away with, not torment them in such measly ways.

RICK
I must talk about your horns, as well.

KRAMPUS
(Chuckles.)
Okay, if you must.

RICK
I just have to say, your appearance is quite terrifying, and it's the horns that do it.

KRAMPUS
Thank you, Rick, I really appreciate that. I am quite proud of the size of my horn.

RICK
Do you use them in your work, or are they just for the image?

KRAMPUS
Mainly for the image, yeah, I guess. I mean, I have impaled a few hundred people on them, but generally, it's just the threat of them that makes a person scared.

RICK
Do they ever get in the way?

KRAMPUS
Well, I avoid going into china shops, let's put it that way. I did have an unfortunate moment when I was a child when I knocked over a very expensive exhibit in a museum, and my mother had to pay for it. I don't ever feel like I'm missing out, though; I mean, I'd much rather have them there than not.

RICK
You tend to wear rags as well. I imagine someone in your line of work can afford much greater clothing, I was just wondering whether that was for image.

KRAMPUS

I'll be honest, these are just my work clothes. I mean, no one who works at McDonalds will wear their uniform when they aren't at work, and I'm just like them, I guess. In the evenings, or the day if I'm working nights, I'll be wearing t-shirt and jeans, maybe the occasional tracksuit bottoms. It really is important to have the right image when I'm inciting fear and committing bloody murder.

RICK

That makes sense, I guess I never really thought about it.

KRAMPUS

Of course you wouldn't, but it does makes sense. No one wants to be slaughtered by a guy in his pyjamas, do they?

RICK

Of course not. I mean, I'm an author, so I work in my pyjamas, you know?

KRAMPUS

(Chuckles.)

Yes, well it's all right for some, isn't it?

RICK

Quite, quite. Well, it's been lovely talking to you.

KRAMPUS

You're welcome, thank you for having me. I'm honoured to be a part of your book.

RICK

And are you working tonight?

KRAMPUS
Yes, just a little. I have a few children to steal for being ungrateful for their presents, and a man who shouted at his cat at Christmas that I need to split in half. You know, just a few things, I don't expect it to be a late one.

RICK
Well, it's been delightful talking to you.

KRAMPUS
Quite.

RICK
Thank you.

KRAMPUS
Thank you, Rick, and good luck with the book.

'TWAS THE NIGHT BEFORE MURDER PART TWO

'Twas the night before Christmas, roughly a year after,
365 long days since Santa's massacre,
The elves and reindeers left slaughtered in blood,
Now Santa lives in jail like the psycho should,
But a creature is stirring far greater than mice,
The beast rages in Kris Kringle on Christmas night,
So when all is quiet, he busts out of his cage,
And returns to the elves with his eyes full of rage,

"How could you convict me you elvish scum?"
he said, as he attacked them all, every single one.
He hung them up by their ears, oh what a sight!
While his cackles and laughs rang out through the night,
He said to one elf, "oh vengeance is sweet,"
And bit off all the toes on their little feet,
By the time he was done there were no elves left,
But something drew his attention that made him feel bereft,

At the edge of the workhouse was a familiar grave, of course,

A stone that belonged to the late Mrs Clause,
Struck down in her prime and taken too soon,
Santa almost regretted putting her in this tomb,
Then he remembered how she nagged every night,
How he'd make a comment and wait for her to bite,
And so he turned his back to the wife he'd left in pieces,
Pulled down his pants and covered her tombstone in faeces.

Then he turned to all the children of the world,
Every hopeful boy and every bright-eyed girl,
They were still expecting gifts under their tree this year,
So he made the decision to spread his own Christmas cheer,
He found the old sleigh and unveiled its glory,
Gave a "ho, ho, ho," and started this year's story,
"You think last year was bad?" he boomed from his chest,
"Then get yourselves ready for this year's mess!"

Midnight struck and he landed in York,
He'd start at the Jone's this year, he thought,
Such a nice family, all happy and sweet,
Middle class parents and children so neat,
He woke them up and brought them downstairs,
They all crept in smiling, and sat on their chairs,
Then he lay the father down for his family to see,
Said "open up" and performed a colonic with the tree,

"Oh Santa," cried the mum, finding it too scary,
So Santa pulled out the tree – missing the fairy,
And force-fed the children milk and mince pies,
Asking repeatedly "you think this is nice?"
Then he turned to the mum and said, "Your turn, my dear,"
She looked to her family, stricken with fear,
Santa bent her over and counted to thirty,

Whilst grabbing sage and onion and stuffing her like the turkey.

In the next house along he didn't make his presence known,
Instead he crept through and stole every phone,
Ate the chocolate that won't make him any thinner,
Whilst peeing all over tomorrow's Christmas dinner,
He removed all the light bulbs and turned back all the clocks,
Hid the TV remote and put spiders in their socks,
And then before he went, before the dog began to bark,
He unpacked all the Lego so they'd step on it in the dark.

In the last few houses he left in every child's stocking,
Pieces of elves he knew would be shocking,
How will little Timmy feel in the morning,
To pull out an elf's finger before he's even finished yawning?
To reach in further whilst watched by his dad Roger,
And pull out an elf's nose, liver, and todger;
How would you feel watching your little kids,
Pulling out parts of elves, bits after bits?

It reached morning and he knew he had won,
He hovered above on his sleigh looking down at what he'd done,
Shouted out to the world, "Now do you see,
What happens if you dare to incarcerate me?"
Then he turned away and aimed for the moon,
Knowing the kids will wake up fairly soon,
So as he flew away, he bellowed out with all his might,
"Merry Christmas to all, and to all a bloody night!"

THE PRESENT: PENULTIMATE CHRISTMAS

He looks up at me from his place between my feet, beside the roaring fire of the log cabin, his beady little eyes making him all the more endearing.

He's all I have in the world. A Yorkshire terrier, my wife's favourite breed.

Well, it was my wife's favourite breed.

I've done what I had to do, and removed myself from society. There is no one alive for miles around. That's not just because of the snowstorm, though that does help to become a recluse; it was my journey to an Alaskan town in the middle of nowhere that has allowed me this solace.

Whatever is in that present, it's following me. It's taken my wife and son, and now...

Now the only person the present can take is myself; I am no longer risking the lives of those I love. It can't get anyone else while I'm here. And if it comes to me, then I will give it hell.

I glance at my shotgun perched against the empty chair opposite, loaded and cocked, ready to blow that gift to smithereens. Let's see how it survives a few blasts. Let's see it try to hurt me now.

Dalton shifts position so his head rests on my slipper. That's his name, by the way – Dalton. I named him after my favourite James Bond actor, Timothy Dalton. Some of the

James Bond films he was in were lousy, but he was always okay.

I lean my head back and close my eyes. The snow rages outside, and I don't expect it will end. It's approaching 4.00 a.m. and the darkness of Christmas Day has replaced the darkness of Christmas Eve night.

Once morning arrives, so will the present.

And I will be ready.

But it's not quite morning yet, so I let my eyes rest. My mind rages, but the peace of my solitude calms it, and my thoughts indulge memories of Christmases past.

Bobby. Just a kid. Taken before he reached double figures. He'd brought me Christmas again, and all he'd received was death.

Linda. Childhood sweetheart, lifetime love, and soulmate. A love like her only comes once in a lifetime, and I've had mine, so I guess it's loneliness from here on out.

My mind drifts into a dreamless slumber, awoken hours later by the tap of a branch on the window, and Dalton's barking that follows it. Damn dog seems to think any noise from outside is an intruder.

"It's nothing," I say. "Go back to sleep."

But the tap of the branch comes again, and Dalton is on high alert, ready to defend his territory.

I look over my shoulder. The windowpane is brown and mouldy, and the window is filthy, both inside and out. The branch is only just visible beyond the muck.

It taps again, and Dalton starts growling.

"Quiet!" I snap.

Then a branch taps a window in another room, and he sprints through the hallway and out of sight, barking at it, warning that branch that it won't be coming into his home!

"Bloody dog," I say and lean my head back, closing my eyes to the sound of his distant barking.

It's incessant. Non-stop. Over and over, bark after bark.

Then it does stop.

And I enjoy the satisfying silence.

Only, the silence lasts too long, and I begin to wonder where my dog has gone.

"Dalton?" I call.

Nothing.

"Dalton, come here, boy," I say.

Nothing.

I reach for a bag of treats from atop the fireplace and shake them; he can never resist a treat, and he knows that sound.

But he doesn't come.

I glance at the clock. I must have slept for a while, as it's going on ten o'clock.

I push myself from my seat and rattle the bag of treats again.

"Dalton! Dalton, come on!"

Still nothing.

The wind whistles through cracks in the windows, the branches tap harder against the glass, and the snow batters the cabin. Other than that, there is no noise. The cabin is at rest.

I walk through the hallway, my stiff limbs causing me to limp, and I pause, looking into the other room.

"Dalton? Dalton, where are you?"

I walk through to the kitchen, wondering if he's waiting by the back door, wanting to go pee.

But he isn't.

I turn to head back.

That's when I see it.

In the corner of the kitchen. Red and gold wrapping paper. The lid slightly crooked, like it's been opened, like someone's had a look, or a sniff inside.

Shit. Dalton.

"Dalton?" I shout, with more alarm, more terror. "Dalton, where are you, boy? Where are you?"

From the living room I hear a bang, one that makes the cabin shake. Then another. Then another.

Umph. Umph. Umph.

I rush through to find my dog charging at the wall, running his head into the wood, again and again, over and over, taking a few steps back and launching itself so hard it makes the wall shake and the picture frames rattle.

"Stop it!" I say. "Stop it, now!"

Umph. Umph. Umph.

I grab hold of the dog, but he bites my hand. I flinch away, grabbing hold of my wrist, staring at a few spots of blood appearing on my palm, and Dalton continues running at the wall.

Umph. Umph. Umph.

What has gotten into him? He's never so much as growled at me, or bitten me playfully…

I go to grab him again, but he leaps out of my grasp and knocks me to the floor.

I look up at him and he stares back at me, with a resolved look, a look that says *goodbye, old friend.*

"Dalton, no!"

And he turns, runs to the fireplace, and dives onto the flames.

"Dalton!"

His body wriggles and writhes and the smell of burnt meat fills the room. I consider trying to pull him out, but as soon as I put my hand anywhere near the flames, they reach out for me and prompt me to jump back.

I am forced to stand here, watching my dog burn to death. My companion, my replacement for a family, the only friend I have in the world. Gone.

The flames quickly die out once he stops moving, and all I have left are his charred remains.

That present.

That god damn present.

That fucking shitty little present.

I grab the shotgun and charge through the cabin to the kitchen, ready to blast it, ready to destroy it.

But, of course, once I reach the kitchen, all I find is an empty corner where the present was.

A full search of the house finds no sign that the present was ever here.

The Present concludes later in the anthology...

TINY TIM: THE TRAUMA YEARS

"I am not tiny!" Tim shouted for the fifth time that day.

He was twenty-five years old for Christ's sake! He was a partner at Scrooge & Marley, not a little child in a famous book – or an *infamous* book if you asked Tim.

Noticing Tim's exasperation, Ebenezer stepped out of his office and said serenely, "Tim, would you mind if I borrow you for a moment?"

With a glare at the charity collector, Tim marched into Ebenezer's office. Ebenezer gave his donation, wished the man a merry Christmas, and entered his office, closing the door behind him.

"Whatever is the matter?" he asked.

"I'm just fed up of it," Tim replied. "Every year, it's the same thing. Everyone reads that book and starts calling me Tiny Tim again. I'm a grown man now!"

Ebenezer sat down at his desk, slowly and particularly. Everything he did was with purpose and precision, every silence was because he was deep in thought, reflecting on words said and preparing his next sentence.

Tim watched his business partner. Since that Christmas many years ago, when there was miraculous change in him, Ebenezer had been as good as a second father to him, and had been keen to take him on as an apprentice, and eventually promote him to partner. But they both knew Ebenezer didn't have many years left running this place; his hair was completely grey, and he hobbled on a walking stick everywhere he went. He should have retired many years ago.

But Tim knew Ebenezer wouldn't be willing to leave the business in the hands of someone as angry as he. Not until Ebenezer was forced to. And for that reason, Tim wished he could be calmer, could be more like his great mentor – he just struggled every Christmas Eve when people would start referring to him as Tiny Tim again.

"They don't know any better, my friend," Ebenezer said, his voice warm like a calm fire one might hold their cold hands over on a winter night. "Is it worth losing your temper?"

"I know it isn't, I just – it gets so annoying. I hate Christmas."

Ebenezer's eyes widened, just for a second, at this shocking revelation.

"And where does this hatred get you?"

"I don't understand."

"I mean, Timothy, where does this hatred toward this season get you?"

"I don't care. I've had enough of it."

"I once knew a man who said a similar thing."

"Oh, enough, Ebenezer, enough! I've heard this story for years, and I'm not a child anymore, I don't have time for fairy tales."

"It is no fairy tale."

"Well it sure sounds like one."

Tim stood. Turned away from his old friend. Put a hand on his hip, the other on his forehead, and began entertaining thoughts that were quite drastic.

What could he do to the next person to call him Tiny Tim?

No, not what *could* he do – what was he *willing* to do?

How far would he go to show everyone that he was not a child anymore? His illness had been dealt with by the best doctors Ebenezer could find, and Tim had accomplished so much since.

"It is time for me to go," Ebenezer said, standing.

Tim collected Ebenezer's coat and, as Ebenezer approached the door, Tim held it out for him.

"Thank you," Ebenezer said with a smile, and placed his arms in the jacket before collecting his hat and taking his walking stick.

"Will I be seeing you in the morning?"

"I should hope so."

"I'm winning at Charades this year, I promise!"

"Sure." Ebenezer nodded jovially and left the office.

Tim watched Ebenezer out of the foggy window as he turned the corner and proceeded down the snowy streets of London.

Almost as soon as Ebenezer was out of sight, there was a knock on the door. Tim opened the door to a carol singer, who sang a rendition of *Joy to the World*. Tim stood back and enjoyed the temporary escape from a world he was growing tired of.

Once the young boy finished, he gazed up at Tim and said, "Penny for the song?"

"Why, of course."

"Wait – do I know you?"

"Excuse me? I don't believe we've met."

"You're Tiny Tim, aren't you!"

Tim glared at the boy with a rage that started from his belly, and rose through him.

"Hey, that's Tiny Tim!" said another voice from across the street.

"Oh, yeah, Tiny Tim, that little boy in the story!" said another.

Tim growled.

Enough was enough.

And, as the carol singer said, "You don't look so tiny anymore," he snapped, and his wrath was unleashed.

※

Ebenezer awoke on Christmas morning, lost in thought. He felt bad about leaving Tim alone, but he was growing old, and he didn't have the energy he used to. There was a time when he would take Tim on a long walk full of reflection and discussion, and would guide him to the conclusions that would mean he'd cope with this troublesome world far better than Ebenezer did when he was younger.

But Ebenezer was tired, and not just in his body, but also in his mind. He could feel the end drawing near, and he wasn't sure if he would see many more Christmases.

Even so, Tim was in need of guidance, and that was why he'd beseeched the ghosts to visit him last night. He had encouraged them to teach Tim about his Christmas past, present and future, in hope that Tim could learn the same lessons he did. They had agreed that such a task was essential, and the first ghost went to Tim's home to wait.

Ebenezer was quite looking forward to discussing it with Tim once he arrived at his home.

He dressed himself in his finest, with tails and top hat,

and readied himself to see the world. His house was large, which meant it was empty, and he was looking forward to being somewhere crammed with joy.

With a smile and a leap, he left his house and tipped his hat at the first lady to walk past, and tipped it at a child and a gentleman too, greeting them each with a simple, "Merry Christmas."

This morning didn't feel as vibrant as Christmas morning normally did, however. The buzz in the air wasn't quite so vibrant, and there didn't seem to be many people about.

That was, until he turned the corner, where he was to walk past his office on the way to Tim's. There was a large group of people there, quite a few actually, and it took Ebenezer a moment to realise they were gathered around his office door.

A police officer rushed past him, his baton at the ready, shouting at all the voyeurs to move out of the way. Ebenezer used the parting of the crowd caused by the police officer to follow.

There, on the step, was a man Ebenezer barely recognised. Yet, beneath the bloody exterior, he knew this man to be Tim; there was no mistaking it.

By his feet was a young boy, one Ebenezer remembered carol singing at his door last year, with his throat sliced, atop another few bodies in similar condition.

The police officer hoisted Tim to his feet, at which point his feeble eyes lifted and noticed Ebenezer. His reaction was delayed, and he seemed quite lethargic, but he clearly recognised him.

"Why, Tim, whatever happened?"

"I'm sorry, Ebenezer," was all he could say.

"But – but did you not arrive home last night?"

Tim shook his head. "I was here."

"And the ghosts?"

"What ghosts? That's just a made-up story..."

The police officer dragged the young man away, leaving Ebenezer to stare at the mess.

If only Tim had gone home. If only those ghosts could have spoken to him. If only...

It did make Ebenezer wonder, however, what would have happened if he'd never had his experience with the ghosts. Maybe he would have committed such atrocities as well.

Then again, without the change the ghosts inspired in Ebenezer, Tim wouldn't have survived, and this mess wouldn't have been created.

He imagined Tim's Christmas future will be behind bars now. If he isn't hanged, that is.

Oh, Tiny Tim.

What fools we are.

A LETTER FROM SIMON

Dear Santa,

I must say what a delight it was to receive your gifts last year. I imagined many of the items I requested being met with scepticism, but when I unveiled the large box left beneath my Christmas shrub to discover an elf, shackled to a pole, adorned in a bondage mask, I don't think I could have been more content.

Of course, this year I have a new list, and one that I am rather enthused about. Should you also wish to deliver me a present this year, then I would be thrilled to find any of these items presented to me on Christmas morning.

Oh, and I should mention, I am writing this letter with my new dictation software! It types out everything I say and it is just marvellous, it even, oh, what, hang on I

ah my god let me out please just let me go I won't tell anyone please just mmph mmmmm aah glurg

Apologies. As I was saying, please find attached my list for your perusal. I hope you find the items satisfactory, and sufficient enough to prompt you with ideas for what to supply me with on Christmas morning.

Oh, and Santa, do be discreet when delivering said gift. The woman tied up in my kitchen tends to make a raucous noise when she hears even the tiniest creak of the floorboard, and I wouldn't want to be woken whilst you are attempting to be inconspicuous.

My list is as follows:

A Jamie Oliver Cookbook. (By this I don't mean a cookbook by Jamie Oliver, but a cookbook about how to cook Jamie Oliver. Please note the difference between the two, as I wouldn't want semantics to ruin my festive period.)

A cross between a Darth Vader mask and a gimp mask. Honestly, imagine it – it just looks right.

A copy of Donald Trump's manifesto. I keep running out of toilet paper.

That girl with the dimple who gets on the bus with me in the morning. Failing that, just her dimple; do with the rest of her as you wish.

A McDonalds that uses its rude employees for burger meat. I feel this consequence would result in much better service.

A copy of *Pride and Prejudice* in case Donald Trump's manifesto isn't big enough.

The true identity of Jack the Ripper. And a time machine if possible, as I feel like we'd get on.

My ex-wife's spleen. It's the one part of her I miss.

A child possessed by the devil and their exorcist. (Honestly, not too bothered about the exorcist, as he'll only be there in case we get hungry.)

Death to any girl who sings *All I Want For Christmas Is You* at their Christmas talent show. I mean for Christ's sake, pick another song.

A rusty nutcracker.

Your nuts, to go with the previous present.

A woman with the sexual appetite of an eighteen-year-old boy. Failing that, an eighteen-year-old boy in a wig – I'm aware I can't have everything I desire.

The head of whoever cast Russell Crowe in Les Misérables. I mean, seriously? It's a musical, what were you thinking?

The woman I saw in Wetherspoons the other day. The waiter brought four hot plates balanced on his arms to the wrong table and, whilst struggling with these plates, the customer said "it's not ours but we'll have it if it's free" then laughed like it was the funniest thing anyone has ever said. I would like her to be disembowelled please.

A crucifix with that bleeding fella on it. In fact, don't bother with the crucifix, just give me the bleeding fella. And, while you're at it, make him real. In fact, it doesn't even have to be a fella, just make sure they're bleeding.

Your wife, wearing your Santa outfit and a Teletubby mask. I trust I do not need to explain my reasons.

Alternatively, your wife wearing a Teletubby outfit and a Santa mask. Again, I trust explanations will not be necessary.

An elf in a tutu. Once again, explanations are not required.

A shark with laser beams attached to its head and a highly trained ninja. (I just want to see which one will win!)

The head of anyone who uses the word *moist*.

Also, the head of anyone called Keith. It's a horrid name, and I would like to start phasing it out.

Whilst we're at it, I'll also have the head of anyone who names their children something like Destiny or Wisdom or Justice or River or Essence. Just give your child a proper name for fuck's sake.

A copy of *Psycho B*tches* by Rick Wood. He's a wonderfully spectacular author, that man – and very modest about it too.

The love of a good woman. Failing that, the intestines of a good woman.

And, finally, do get something for yourself. A bottle of mead, perhaps, or a torture kit to use on Mrs Claus. I hear chainsaws are coming back, which might be something to consider.

With all my season's greetings,
    Yours,
    Simon.
    (The Christmas Cannibal)

THE PRESENT: THE FINAL CHRISTMAS

THE FOUR WALLS ARE PADDED, and I enjoy bouncing off them, but they are not my home.

"It is for now," my therapist says as he injects me with something; Prozac I reckon, but I'm not entirely sure.

"But it's Christmas today," I tell him.

"It is," he says with a smile, an endearing smile, like a daddy reading a story or a friend offering a cake.

"And the present..."

"What about the present?"

"It's coming today..."

"You've spoken a lot about this present – what actually is it?"

I gasp. Put my finger over my lips. Shush him.

Mustn't tell, mustn't know.

The present will arrive in good time, yes, it will, it will arrive, but you don't know where it will be, no you don't – you have to wait.

Be patient.

"You don't believe me, do you?" I say, turning my eyes from him to the wall to him to the wall and widening them so the eye floaters that cross my vision line up with the corner of the room.

"I believe that you believe it."

I laugh. Cackle. Hah! What a line.

I believe that you believe it you believe it if you believe it well if I believe it don't you believe it we could all believe it if we believed it but I believe it I believe it I believe it believe it believe it believeitbelieveitbelieveitbelieveit.

Oh my, I do think it's supper time.

No, breakfast comes in the morning, silly.

Breakfast.

In the morning.

Then gifts.

You always open gifts in the morning...

Believe it.

Believe it.

Believe it.

Believe it.

Believe it.

Believe it.

Believe it.

Believe it.

Believe it.

Believe it.

Believe it.

Believe it.

Believe it.

Believe it.

Believe it.

Believe it.

Believe it.

Believe it.

Believe it.

Believe it.

Believe it.

Believe it.

Believe it.

Believe it.

Believe it.
Believe it.
Believe it.
Believe it.
Believe it.
Believe it.
Believe it.
Believe it.
Believe it.
Believe it.
Believe it.
Believe it.
Believe it.
Believe it.
Believe it.
Believe it.
Believe it.
Believe it.
Believe it.
Believe it.
Believe it.
Believe it.
Believe it.
Believe it.
Believe it.
Believe it.
Believe it.
Believe it.
Believe it.
Believe it.
Believe it.
Believe it.
Believe it.
Believe it.
Believe it.
Believe it.

Believe it.
Believe it.
Believe it.
Believe it.
Believe it.

"And who gives you this present?"

SOMEONE TALKS!

Who is this man with a beard and glasses and clipboard and pen. He is certainly not Santa.

Santa does not bring this present.

Santa doesn't bring any presents, only hope, only hope my friends my children, only hope to boys and girls around the world so LONG AS YOU BELIEVE THE LIE THE FUCKING LIE.

"Why," I answer, "I do declare that I do not know."

"I see."

"YOU SEE?"

Of course you see you wear glasses you fool you see very well with those on you do you do you do.

Where am I?

I'm not in my padded cell now, no I'm not, because there are no pads and there are no cells but my arms are in this straitjacket they are they are they are indeed.

A man in white walks behind me and in front of me but they are two different men you see, not the same, they just crossed at the same time.

"You lost your son and wife at Christmas, did you not?"

"And my dog."

Don't forget the dog you fucking nazi, do not forget Dalton oh Dalton oh Dalton my dear Dalton...

"And this was because of this... present?"

"Yes it was it was indeed it was."

"And do you expect to see this present this morning?"

I look at him.

Tilt my head.

Tilt it further.

And scream.

HOW DARE YOU you cretin HOW DARE YOU bring up the present HOW DARE YOU abuse me so HOW DARE YOU ask!

He tells a man to take me back to my cell and he manhandles me and I tell him to go fuck his mother and he drags me through and I tell him to go fuck his aunt and he drags me through I tell him, tell him, tell him nothing because he's no longer there.

He throws me in my cell and closes the wall, and there are four walls, four walls again, all padded, and...

What's this?

In the corner of my padded cell...

A present.

Red and gold.

I creep toward it.

Sniff it.

It doesn't smell of anything.

But it's the present that killed my son.

But it's the present that killed my wife.

But it's the present that killed my DOG OH MY DOG MY DEAR DEAR DOG.

And finally, after all these years, I am going to see inside of it, I am going to see what it is.

My hands are free now. How are they free? They must have taken the straitjacket off.

I peel the lid up, slightly, waiting to see if I hear anything or smell anything or hear anything or smell anything.

Nothing.

It is dark inside the present.

I throw the lid off completely, discarding it across the room.

Inside it is a smaller package, a much smaller package, one wrapped in tin foil, a smaller package wrapped in tin foil that I take out and hold in my hands.

I bend it.

It's a book.

I know it is. It's a book.

I open it, peeling the corner at first, then the next corner.

Part of the cover is revealed. I see the word Twelve.

Twelve twelve twelve twelve twelve twelve twelve twelve twelve twelve twelve twelve.

I pull away the tin foil, shredding it, discarding it.

I fall to my knees and scream as I see the cover.

And I read its name.

It can't be, it can't, it can't...

But it is.

And I read the name aloud.

"Twelve Days..."

I can't get it all out in one, so I gulp, I take a breath, and I read it.

"Twelve Days of Christmas Horror."

But there's more. Another line. And it says...

"Volume Two."

Oh dear God.

I scream. Harder. Louder. I run against the wall, pounding my head into it, ramming into it. Bellowing, roaring, destroying my lungs with the strength of my scream.

They come running in and restrain me. I try and tell them about the present but it's gone.

But I know.

I know.

It was the most monstrous thing I've ever seen, and the worst present ever oh yes it was the worst it was it was.

And, as they place a sedative in my neck, and I fall asleep, I drift away, never to wake up again, wishing I'd left it at volume one.

Oh, how I wish I hadn't read that book...

Now I am doomed.

As is anyone else who reaches its final word.

JOIN RICK WOOD'S READER'S GROUP...

And get his horror anthology **Roses Are Red So Is Your Blood** for free!

Join at **www.rickwoodwriter.com/sign-up**

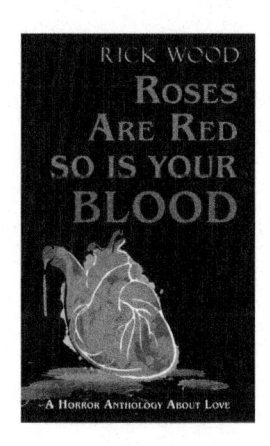

ALSO AVAILABLE BY RICK WOOD

RICK WOOD

TWELVE DAYS OF CHRISTMAS HORROR

BLOOD SPLATTER BOOKS

18+

This Book Is Full of BODIES

Rick Wood

BLOOD SPLATTER BOOKS

18+

PSYCHO B*TCHES

RICK WOOD

BOOK ONE IN THE SENSITIVES SERIES

THE SENSITIVES

RICK WOOD

BLOOD SPLATTER BOOKS

18+

SHUTTER HOUSE

RICK WOOD

BLOOD SPLATTER BOOKS

18+

HOME INVASION

Rick Wood

BLOOD SPLATTER BOOKS

18+

WOMAN SCORNED

RICK WOOD

Printed in Great Britain
by Amazon